STORYLAND

Classic Tales for Children

II

Retold by Jane Carruth

Illustrated by Rene Cloke

AWARD PUBLICATIONS

The Ugly Duckling

It was summer and all the fields and meadows were green. Flowers grew close to the riverbank where a Mother Duck was sitting in her nest.

Mother Duck had been sitting on her eggs for a long time and she was growing very tired. "How much longer must I sit?" she asked herself again and again.

Presently one of her oldest friends from the farmyard came to visit her.

"Quack! Quack!" she exclaimed, when Mother Duck showed her the eggs. "You have a monster egg in the nest, I do declare! It looks like a turkey egg. Why," she went on, peering closely at the egg, "it's twice as big as any of the others!"

After her friend had gone, Mother Duck
went back to the nest. To her great delight
the eggs began to crack, one by one, and
she was soon the proud mother of six pretty
yellow ducklings.

"What a splendid bunch!" Mother Duck
said aloud. "All perfect and full of high
spirits – just like me when I was young!
I will have to think of
some really nice names
to give all of them."

There was now only the big, monster
egg left in the nest. When it finally
cracked open Mother Duck was very upset.
   "Quack! Quack! Quack!" she cried, at
the sight of her youngest. "He can't be
mine. He is far too big and ugly!"
   The youngest of her ducklings was so
big and ugly compared to his brothers
and sisters that poor Mother Duck bowed
her head in shame as he stood before her.

The next day Mother Duck set off
for the river. Soon all her babies were
swimming after her, and she could not
help feeling pleased and proud. To her
surprise, the Ugly Duckling proved to be
an excellent swimmer.

"He is more at home in the water than
his brothers and
sisters," Mother
Duck told herself,
as she watched.

After their swim, Mother Duck took
the path to the farmyard with her children
waddling behind. "You must all be on
your best behaviour," she warned them,
when the farm came in sight. "I am taking
you to meet the Dowager Duck. She is
the most important person in the farmyard. She will soon make up her mind
about you all..."

Alas, the visit was not a success.
"I cannot congratulate you," said the
Dowager Duck to Mother Duck. "Six of
your little ones are pretty enough, but
that strange ugly boy has no place here."

"I agree with you, Dowager," gobbled the fiery Turkey Cock, deciding to take part in the conversation. "Never set eyes on such an odd creature before..."

When she heard this, one of the hens aimed a very spiteful peck at the poor duckling.

From that moment, the Ugly Duckling
led a miserable life. The milkmaid
usually tried to kick him whenever she
passed, and the hens chased him.

Even his brothers
and sisters made
fun of him.

The Ugly Duckling was so lonely and unhappy that he made up his mind to run away. "Nobody will miss me," he told himself sadly, as he left the farmyard early one morning.

He could not walk or fly very fast but somehow he reached the great marsh. The marsh was where the wild ducks lived, and soon one of them flew down to greet him.

"Who are you? Where do you come from?" the wild duck demanded. "You are very ugly!"

The Ugly Duckling hoped the wild ducks would let him stay with them. But one day as he watched them fly over the marsh, there was a loud BANG and one of them dropped out of the sky.

Soon after the loud BANG, a big brown dog splashed through the water towards him, mouth open, and the Ugly Duckling went stiff with fright. The big dog did not harm him, but the Duckling knew that he could never make the marsh his home. "I'll go now," he decided.

When it began to get dark,
the little duckling
knew he couldn't go
much further.

In the moonlight he saw a little house
that looked so inviting that he began to
think about food and shelter for the night.
"I might even be allowed to stay," he
thought, as he went up to the door.

An old woman with a hen on her shoulder
and a cat at her side opened the door and
invited him inside. "You are welcome to
stay as long as you like," she said kindly,
"so long as you lay me an egg every day..."
Her kind words made the duckling very happy.

But the old woman was only pretending to like the Ugly Duckling. When she found he could not lay eggs, she shouted at him and chased him with her broom. Her cat teased him and her hen pecked him. One day the cat hissed at him, "Stupid, ugly creature. Go away." And the hen clacked, "Why don't you leave us? We don't want you here."

By now the duckling was so miserable that the very next morning he slipped away.

There was no one to say goodbye to the Ugly Duckling or to wish him luck. He felt so sad and lonely that he wished he could die.

That day he rested very little until at last he came to a pond. As soon as he was in the water he swam and dived and began to feel less lonely.

"I shall stay here for ever and ever," he told himself. But soon the nights grew cold and the leaves on the trees changed to brown and yellow and then dropped to the hard earth.

Just before the first snowflakes fell, the duckling looked up into the grey, wintry sky and saw some beautiful white birds with long, graceful necks flying overhead. "Oh, how beautiful they are!" the Ugly Duckling cried. "If only I could look like they do!"

The duckling could not forget the beautiful birds, not even when an icy wind began to freeze the water. Up and down he swam but the ice closed in all round him. One morning he found he was trapped in the ice and could not move.

He would have died if a farmer had not come by the pond. "Poor, little chap," he said. "I can't leave you here to die!" And he broke the ice with his stout

wooden clog. Already half-dead the
poor duckling had no strength to struggle
though he was very frightened.

"There!" said the man in a kindly
voice. "I'll carry you home under my
jacket. It will shelter you from the
bitter wind."

The farmer was poor but he was
certain his wife would take care of the
duckling until he grew stronger.

As soon as he was home, he called his wife, and she took hold of the duckling and held him gently.

"Of course we'll keep him," she said. "He can stay in the farmhouse until he is strong enough to fly."

"What about the children?" her husband asked. "Will they be kind to him I wonder?"

Alas, the children were not kind to
the poor duckling. They tried to play
a game with him, chasing him round and
round the big farm kitchen.

The Ugly Duckling was so scared that
he flew into the milk-churn, upsetting
the milk all over the floor.

"Leave him to me!"
shrieked the girl.
"I'll catch him!"
shouted the boy.

Their mother was so furious by now that she tried to grab hold of the duckling.

Terrified, he crashed into the butter-churn. At this the children laughed louder than ever.

The poor, frightened duckling was so dazed that he scarcely knew where he was.

The terrified duckling was almost caught by the boy as he made a frantic dash through the half-open kitchen door. When he found himself outside, he used his remaining strength to escape across the snow-covered field.

Somehow or other he managed to live through the long hard winter making use of whatever shelter he could find.

One morning, in the warm Spring sunshine, the Ugly Duckling felt a new strength in his wings. "Now I can really go into the wide, wide world," he told himself, as he rose into the air and flew away over the moors.

After a time he came to rest in a pretty scented garden, and there on the lake were some beautiful white swans!

The Ugly Duckling was filled with joy at the sight of them. "Even if they kill me because I am so ugly," he thought. "What does it matter?" and he flew on to the lake and swam towards the stately birds.

"Kill me, if you must!" cried the poor duckling, bending his head.

Something strange and wonderful happened then. The Ugly Duckling saw himself reflected in the clear water. And lo and behold! He was no longer the ugly, grey bird that everybody hated but a graceful white swan!

Presently, two little children came to the lake to feed the swans. They began throwing bread into the water, and the girl cried, "Look! A new swan! and the new one is the youngest and the most beautiful of all!"

Cinderella

Once upon a time there was a rich
merchant who, when his first wife died,
married again, hoping that his new wife
and her two daughters would take care
of his only child when he was abroad.

"You can forget your own name," the
sisters said spitefully when they found
themselves alone with the merchant's
daughter. "From now on, we mean to call

you Cinderella! Your place is in the
kitchen among the cinders."

So Cinderella became a servant in the
big house, cleaning and scrubbing all
day long. And never did she get a word
of thanks from any one.

Usually the two sisters were bad-
tempered, but when the Royal Invitation
came one day from the Palace they rushed
into the kitchen to tell Cinderella.

Splendid new gowns were ordered and when they arrived, Cinderella was told to help with the fittings. How she longed to go to the Ball and dance with the Prince! It was only an impossible dream and when she dared speak about it, her stepsisters teased her and laughed at her right up to the moment they went off to the Palace.

Cinderella was all alone in the dark kitchen, wishing with all her heart she could go to the Ball, when there was a flash of light and a lady stood before her.

In her hand was a silver wand, which did not surprise Cinderella. "I am your very own Fairy Godmother," she said in a gentle voice. "I can make your wish come true!"

It was just as if the wonderful Fairy was reading Cinderella's thoughts for now she

was smiling sweetly as she went on, "Take me into the garden, child, and show me the biggest pumpkin."

Without a word, Cinderella obeyed.

The Fairy took the round, yellow pumpkin and touched it with her wand. It changed at once into a splendid golden coach, and the Fairy turned to Cinderella: "This coach will take you to the Ball," she smiled. "Did I not say I could make wishes come true! Now, fetch me that big mousetrap I saw near the door."

Cinderella gasped as her Godmother changed the two white mice in the trap into two handsome, white horses. It was then the turn of a fat long-whiskered rat to be turned into a fat jolly coachman. And a pair of lizards, at the touch of the magic wand, became two very grand footmen in handsome uniforms.

Cinderella hung her head when the Fairy
told her that her coach was waiting. "How
can I go to the Ball in rags?" she cried.
"I'd look a proper Cinders!"

Her Godmother smiled as, with a wave of
her wand, she changed Cinders' rags into
a gown of shimmering satin.

Then the Fairy gave her a pair of dainty glass slippers. "Now you are ready to go to the Ball," she said. "But there is one thing you must be sure to remember," she added in a stern voice, as she helped Cinderella into her golden coach. "You must leave before the clock strikes twelve. If you do not, your ball-gown will change to rags, your coach into a pumpkin, and all will be as it once was!"

As soon as Cinderella entered the vast ballroom, lit by a thousand lamps, the Prince saw her and fell instantly in love with her. He did not know her name but he would dance with no one else. And Cinderella was so happy that she forgot all about the time. Light as thistledown in the Prince's arms, she seemed to float round the room.

"Who can she be?" one Ugly Sister whispered to the other from behind her fan. "She must be a Princess!"

"She's one of these high-born Princesses from a far country," came the reply. "The Prince will never notice us now," she added bitterly.

All around the glittering ballroom the lords and ladies were talking about the lovely stranger. Everyone was trying to make a guess as to which country she came from.

The Prince was so enchanted with his
beautiful partner that he insisted she
dance every dance with him.

And Cinderella, by now, was so in
love with the Prince that she only wished
to please him.

She was having such a wonderful time
that she forgot all about the Fairy's
warning – until she heard the Palace clock
strike twelve.

Without a word to the Prince, she fled
from the ballroom, and down the great
marble staircase.

In her haste, one of her glass slippers
came off, but she did not dare to stop
and pick it up.

Long before she reached the Palace
gates, her wonderful ball-gown had changed
into her old ragged dress.

There was no golden coach waiting to
carry her through the dark streets. No
jolly coachman to greet her before
urging his white horses into a trot. No
grand footmen. All had vanished!

"If only I had remembered!" Cinderella
thought, as she began to walk home.

Somehow she wasn't greatly surprised when she came upon the large, yellow pumpkin by the roadside. Two little mice were scampering about, and running away fast was a fat, brown rat with long shining whiskers. Only the two, slow-moving lizards seemed to have nowhere to go, and she began to wonder if they had enjoyed being two grand footmen. "Perhaps they liked being footmen better than they liked being lizards," she thought, as she watched them. "I know which I'd rather be."

The next morning, the Ugly Sisters couldn't stop talking about the Ball and the lovely Princess who had captured the Prince's heart. Cinderella was busy dusting and sweeping but

she could not help smiling to herself as she heard what they had to say about the beautiful Princess from a far country. "We mustn't blame the Prince for not dancing with us," they said at last. "She was so beautiful."

That same week, a Herald was seen in the street. Every now and then he rang a bell and read from a white scroll.

"Listen, all ye good people. His Royal Highness, the Prince, wishes it to be known that the girl who can wear the glass slipper that was found on the night of the Ball will be his royal bride."

No wonder the page carried the velvet cushion with such care! On it rested the

dainty glass slipper. Every house in the
town was visited. At last, the Herald came
to the house where the Ugly Sisters lived.

"I am sure that slipper will fit my foot!"
cried one sister. But her foot was much
too big and the other sister laughed loudly.

"Now let me try," she exclaimed. But no
matter how she pushed and pulled, the slipper
would not go on!

At last the royal messenger asked if anyone else lived in the house.

"Only our servant girl, Cinderella!" came the reply.

"Then fetch her here," said the royal messenger in a stern voice. "She must be allowed to try on the glass slipper."

To the amazement of all watching, the glass slipper fitted Cinderella's small foot perfectly.

Trembling with rage, the sisters
ordered Cinderella to go back into her
kitchen. Before she could obey, her kind
Fairy Godmother appeared and touched her
with her magic wand, changing her into the
lovely Princess of the Ball.

Soon, by some trick of magic which the Fairy refused to explain, the Prince himself appeared and took Cinderella into his arms. In a voice full of joy, he begged her to return to the Palace with him. "We shall soon be married," he vowed.

The Ugly Sisters did their best to pretend that they, too, were full of joy at Cinderella's new-found happiness. And Cinderella, being a nice, forgiving girl, saw to it that they received a special invitation to her wedding!

Jack and the Beanstalk

There was once a boy called Jack.
Jack lived in the country with his
mother and helped her to look after the
hens and their gentle, good-tempered cow.

One day, as she was feeding the hens,
his mother said to him, "Ever since your
poor father died we have been short of
money. Now there is scarcely enough to
pay next month's rent."

"Well, we still have our faithful Blossom," Jack replied cheerfully. "She never fails to give us milk."

His mother said nothing more but the next morning she told Jack that he must take Blossom to market.

"What!" Jack cried. "We can't sell Blossom, Mother!"

Alas, that same day saw Jack setting off for market, leading Blossom.

He had not gone far down the road when he met an odd little man. "Hello, Jack," said the little man. "Where are you going with that fine cow?"

"I'm taking Blossom to market to sell her," Jack said sadly.

"You'll make a better bargain if you sell her to me for these," said the man, dropping some brightly coloured beans into Jack's hat. "Plant them tonight and

they will make your fortune. Yes,
my magic beans will make your fortune."

At the word 'magic' Jack's eyes began
to shine. "It's a bargain!" he cried.

Jack's mother was so angry when she
heard about the bargain her son had made
that she sent him off to bed without any
supper, and she threw the beans out of the
window before bursting into tears.

Jack woke early the next morning
and went to the window. He gasped with
surprise when he saw that an enormous,

gigantic tree had taken root and grown in
the night while he slept. It was so huge
that its topmost branches reached into the
sky. "So the little man's beans were
magic!" Jack thought. "He didn't try to
cheat me. And now they've grown and grown
into a great, tall, magic beanstalk!"

Jack stared up at the magic beanstalk
for a long time before he turned back into
his bedroom. He knew now what he must do!

His fingers were all thumbs as he began
to dress. When he was ready at last he
rushed outside and began to climb the magic
beanstalk. It was easier than he had
imagined and when he glanced down, the
farm look like a tiny doll's house.

Up and up he climbed until he found the
very tallest branches of the beanstalk
were bathed in swirling white clouds.

When he reached the very top Jack saw
a long white road stretching before him
and, at the end of it, a tall castle with
many turrets. The mysterious castle seemed
to beckon Jack and, without hesitating, he
set off down the long white road.

He was so excited that he did not
think of any danger. Here was an adventure
after his own heart!

"I'm ready for anything!" he told himself.

As soon as he reached the castle, Jack
went up to the stout wooden door and
stretched up to use the big brass knocker.
There was no answer to his knocking for
some time and he began to wonder if the
owner of the castle was away from home.
Disappointed he was about to turn away

when suddenly the door
opened and a woman came
out to greet him. She
was so big and tall
that poor Jack felt like a dwarf.

"Please can I come in?"
Jack said, when he could
find his voice. "I am
ever so hungry. Do you
think you could find me
something to eat?"

The woman smiled as she looked down on
Jack. Then she said, "Come in. It is
lucky that my husband is out. He would eat
a boy like you for breakfast!"

Soon Jack was enjoying a bowl of sweet
porridge. As he ate, he forgot about the
fierce giant until the woman suddenly
whispered, "Quick! Hide! He's coming!"

Quick as a flash Jack jumped into the
big stone oven seconds before the giant
thudded into the kitchen. Then in a
great rumbling voice,
he began to roar,
"Fee-fi-fo-fum,
I smell the blood
of an Englishman.

Be he alive,
or be he dead,
I'll grind his
bones to make
my bread.

"No, no, husband," said the giant's
wife. "You smell nothing but the remains
of the venison pie I am keeping for you."
Quickly she put the pie before him and the
giant began to eat huge mouthfuls of the
meat. When his hunger was satisfied, he
called for his wife to bring him his bags
of gold which she did immediately.

From his hiding-place in the oven, Jack
watched the giant begin counting the gold.
Over and over again he counted it until
he was so very weary that he fell fast asleep.

"No wonder," thought Jack, "after all that
pie and those big ham bones." And as
the giant began to snore, Jack made up his
mind to help himself to some of the gold.

As soon as he thought it was safe to leave his hiding-place, he jumped out of the oven and tip-toed towards the sleeping giant. Then, as the giant snored on, Jack snatched one of the bags of gold and ran out of the kitchen without waking the giant.

There was no sign of the giant's wife as he fled down the long stone passage which led to the door. Once outside, Jack took firm hold of the bag of gold and ran as fast as his legs would carry him along the white road. He was out of breath when he reached the beanstalk and began

the long climb down. Down, down, down
he clambered, not without difficulty,
for the bag of gold was heavy and kept
slipping from his grasp.
When Jack reached the ground
at last his mother was there
waiting for him. She was
so pale and anxious that
he cried out, "Don't worry,
Mother, I'm safe, and just
look what I've brought
you! We are rich!"

The giant's gold put an end to all
the worry Jack's mother had. With it she
paid the rent and bought things for the
farm and new clothes for Jack. But
money doesn't last forever and Jack knew,
as he stared up into the beanstalk, that
one day he would climb it again.

"I must find out if the giant has other
treasures," he told his mother one day.
"I must climb the beanstalk just once more
and pay a visit to his castle."

The giant's wife seemed happy to see him
when she answered his knock and soon Jack
was in the huge kitchen and being served
with a delicious bowl of sweet porridge.
There was no sign of the giant until all

at once the ground
beneath Jack's feet
began to shake and
the giant's wife
whispered fearfully,
"It's my husband
come home. Quick,
hide in the oven
as before!" Jack

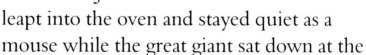

leapt into the oven and stayed quiet as a
mouse while the great giant sat down at the

table and started to eat. Every now and then the giant lifted his head and sniffed the air as he looked round the vast kitchen. But his wife soothed his suspicions with a tasty dish of stewed oxen and after he had eaten it, he called for his magic hen.

Jack watched in amazement as the hen began laying eggs of solid gold. But he waited patiently until the giant fell asleep before daring to snatch the hen and escape from the castle. Alas, the hen began squawk so loudly that the giant awoke and set off in pursuit.

Jack ran like the wind until he came to the beanstalk. Once safely in his own garden, he showed his mother the hen and told her they were now rich. But he could not forget the castle in the clouds and, early one morning, he climbed the magic beanstalk once again.

As before Jack hid in the oven until the giant appeared. And as before he waited patiently until the moment came for the giant to call for his treasure. This time it was a magic harp which filled the vast kitchen with heavenly music.

It was not difficult to take the harp from the sleeping giant but then, as Jack reached the door, it called out "Master! Master!" in a loud voice, waking the giant.

What a chase that was!
The giant was so close
behind Jack that he all
but caught hold of him.
Jack reached the magic

beanstalk first and began clambering down.
"Mother! Mother!" he shouted. "Bring me
the axe. The giant is close behind."

With all his strength, Jack swung the huge axe and the beanstalk began to tremble and shake. Then, suddenly, down it came with a mighty C R A S H – and with it came the giant!

So that was the end of the giant and the end of the magic beanstalk, and all Jack's adventures!

Little Red Riding Hood

One day little Red Riding Hood
and her mummy heard that Grandma was ill.
"You must go to her," said Mummy.

So little Red Riding Hood set off. She carried a basket of fresh eggs and honey and home-made bread for her Grandma.

"I'm glad I'm in my red cloak and hood," she thought, as she skipped along. "I like wearing it because it was Grandma who made it for me."

In fact, she wore it so much that everybody called her Red Riding Hood instead of her proper name!

Little Red Riding Hood's cottage was close to some lonely woods where she was not allowed to play.

Now, Red Riding Hood was thinking more about her sick Grandma than being obedient. And instead of taking the road, she began following the path through the woods.

"I'll get to Grandma's cottage much quicker this way," she thought.

It was lovely in the woods that day!
Soon Red Riding Hood had stopped and was
gathering some pretty blue flowers for her
Grandma. "The flowers will cheer her up,"
she told herself. "And I'll tell her
all about the rabbits and the squirrels
and how friendly they are!"

But there were not only friendly
rabbits and squirrels in the woods that
day! A big, bad, ugly wolf was also out
and about.

As soon as he caught sight of Red
Riding Hood through the trees, he made
up his mind to follow her.

The wolf seemed to be enjoying the sunshine when Red Riding Hood saw him first, and before she had time to run away he spoke. "Good day to you, little girl," he said, in a voice so soft and friendly that Red Riding Hood stopped being frightened.

In a few minutes she had told him
about herself and her sick Grandma in
the cottage on the far side of the wood.
No sooner had the cunning wolf heard about
the old lady than away he ran, and long
before Red Riding Hood could reach the
cottage the wolf was knocking on the door.

"Who is it?"
the old lady
called out in
a weak voice.
"It's your own
Red Riding Hood,"
the wolf replied,
in a low whisper,
hoping to deceive
the old lady. "Then why don't you lift the
latch and come in," the wolf heard her say.

No sooner was that big, bad wolf inside the cottage than he gobbled up the old lady. Then with a wicked snarl, he searched about till he found a bonnet and a shawl which he decided suited him better than some of the others he found in her chest.

After the wolf had admired himself in
the mirror, he went over to the big bed
and hopped in.

Once comfortably settled, he dragged
the sheet right up to his black nose,
pulled the old lady's cap down over his
wicked eyes and waited.

Little Red Riding Hood, unlike the
bad wolf, did not know any short cuts to
her Grandma's cottage. But she ran as
fast as she could until, at last, there
was the cottage.

In answer to her gentle knock came the soft, weak voice of that bad, bad, wolf. "Lift the latch and come right in, child."

Red Riding Hood was smiling as she pushed open the door. "Here I am," she cried. "Wait until you see what Mummy has sent, and all my pretty flowers!"

Red Riding Hood was quite surprised to
see how untidy the cottage was. "Perhaps
poor Grandmamma was too ill to tidy up,"

she said to herself, as she looked towards the big bed. At first, she thought the old lady was asleep, and she put down her basket and took out the eggs and the honey and the home-made bread, before finding a pretty vase for the flowers.

At last she said quietly, "Grandmamma, are you awake?"

"Of course I am, child," a croaky voice answered from the big bed.

"Then let me show you what Mummy has sent," little Red Riding Hood cried. "There's honey and fresh eggs and home-made bread, and I picked some pretty blue flowers for you…" And she began to tip-toe towards the bed.

"Come closer," whispered the wicked wolf. "Come closer and give your old Grandmamma a hug."

"But Grandmamma, what big arms you have got!" she exclaimed.

"All the better to hug you with, my dear," said the wolf.

"And Grandmamma, what big ears you have got!" cried little Red Riding Hood, staring down at the bed.

"All the better to hear you with," said the wolf.

"And Grandmamma," whispered little Red Riding Hood. "What big teeth you have got!"

"All the better to EAT you with!" growled the big, bad wolf.

With that the wolf sprang out of bed, and little Red Riding Hood nearly died of fright. Away she ran, round the room.

Snarling with rage, the old wolf
chased after her. But little Red Riding
Hood was too quick for him.

Just when he was about to catch her,
she managed to escape behind a chair and
the wicked wolf fell flat on his nose.
It was lucky for Red Riding Hood that her

Grandma's nightcap dropped over the wolf's eyes. This gave her the chance to run to the window.

"Help! Help!" she screamed at the top of her voice. "Help! Help! Save me from the wolf!"

Now, working not very far away was a young woodcutter. He knew all about the wicked wolf which sometimes came to the woods so he always kept a sharp look-out.

At first he took Red Riding Hood's screams for the wind whistling in the tall trees. Then he heard the cries again and this time the woodcutter recognised the voice of his little friend, Red Riding Hood. "She must be visiting her old Grandma," he thought, as he set off at a run for the cottage.

It was all over so quickly that Red
Riding Hood could scarcely believe it. The
terrible wolf lay dead, killed by a single
blow of the brave woodcutter's big axe.

"Don't cry," the woodcutter said kindly.
"You are safe now."

"But he has eaten Grandmamma," Red
Riding Hood sobbed. Then she gasped, as
out of the dead wolf stepped Grandmamma!

The greedy wolf had swallowed her whole
and she was almost as good as new –
except for losing her slippers. "Now give
me a kiss and a hug," said she, "and the
woodcutter can take you home."

On the way home, Red Riding Hood told how she had met the wolf. "If I had done what Mummy said, I would never have seen him," she sighed. "Mummy said I must never go into the woods by myself."

"It's always best to do what Mummy says," agreed the woodcutter.

"Even though the big, bad wolf is dead!" little Red Riding Hood exclaimed, beginning to feel happy again.

"Of course!" said the woodcutter, smiling.

Pinocchio

Once upon a time there lived a kind old man called Geppetto. One day a friend gave him a piece of wood shaped like a log.

"I will make a wonderful puppet out of this wood!" Geppetto cried. "We will travel the world together."

When he got home, Geppetto set to work on his puppet. He was clever at carving and had all the right tools.

First he made the head and gave it hair. Then he made the eyes, the nose and the mouth. To his astonishment the eyes began to move and the nose began to grow and the mouth to jeer and laugh.

But nothing could stop Geppetto from finishing his puppet and, as he worked on, he decided to call him Pinocchio. "That is a fine name for a puppet!" he said aloud. "Pinocchio it shall be."

Geppetto was a clever craftsman but even he was surprised how life-like his wonderful puppet was looking. Then suddenly,

without warning, the puppet began to laugh and mock the old man before snatching off his precious wig and dancing all round the room with it.

Now Geppetto loved his little
wooden puppet and wanted to give him
the best. But he had so little money
that he had to sell his coat so that
Pinocchio could go to school. But
Pinocchio went to the Puppet Theatre
instead and climbed on to the stage.

The audience booed and hissed little
Pinocchio for spoiling the Show and the
Puppet Master was furious.

"You'll burn on my fire tonight," he
told Pinocchio. But the puppet begged
so tearfully for his life that the
Puppet Master gave him five gold pieces
before sending him on his way.

On the edge of some woods Pinocchio met Cat and Fox – two desperate villains. Pinocchio foolishly told them all about his gold pieces and Cat and Fox promised to help him take care of them. "We'll meet in the morning," said Fox, with a sly grin. "You can trust us."

When it was nearly dark, Pinocchio was suddenly set upon by two masked robbers. "Your money or your life!" one of them said, in a hoarse whisper.

Pinocchio was so terrified that he did not recognise Cat and Fox. He was sure he was being attacked by two terrible robbers who would have no mercy. But he stayed silent and the villains, with many curses, began shaking him.

Now Pinocchio had hidden his gold
pieces under his tongue and when he
refused to say where they were

104

Cat and Fox tied a rope round his waist and strung him up to the nearest tree.

"You can stay there until you learn some sense," snarled Fox.

"Your gold won't help you now!" hissed Cat in a fury.

Pinocchio watched the robbers depart. He was so scared that he began to wish he had given them his precious gold.

It was lucky for Pinocchio that the
beautiful Blue Fairy Girl took pity on
him and brought him to her little house
on the edge of the woods. She tucked
him up in bed and gave him some of her
magic medicine to drink. But when the
puppet began to tell her lies, the Fairy
touched his nose and made it grow twice
as long and red like a carrot.

Pinocchio soon learnt to love the Blue Fairy but he did not like being told how to behave and one day he ran away. How pleased he was to meet his old friends, Cat and Fox.

"If you bury your gold in a certain field," said Fox, "You will find your fortune is doubled."

Pinocchio buried his gold, closely watched by Cat and Fox and that was the last he ever saw of it!

Pinocchio had many adventures before he went back to the Blue Fairy's little house. "I will stay with her," he said to himself, "and she will teach me how to be good and not tell so many stupid lies."

Alas! When Pinocchio came to the little house, there was a white stone in the garden which said, *"The Blue Fairy lies here. She waited in vain for her little wooden puppet to come back to her."*

Pinocchio burst into tears at the words.

"Dear Blue Fairy," he sobbed, "if you will only come back, I promise to be a good boy. I – I will even go to school..."

No sooner had he said this than the Fairy appeared and took him into her little house. The next day Pinocchio went to school. He sat at a desk with all the other boys but he did not pay attention. All he wanted to do was to go out and play. "I wish I could find a place where there wasn't any school," he told himself.

Now another boy in the class was just as lazy and naughty as Pinocchio. I know a place where you can have fun all day long," he told Pinocchio. "It's called the Land of Donkeys."

A wicked magician ruled over the Land of Donkeys. At first he allowed Pinocchio and his friend to play all the time. Then one day both boys woke up to find they had been changed into grey donkeys, and were up for sale.

Pinocchio was soon sold to a circus but he could not learn any of the tricks and he got in everybody's way. None of the other performers would work with him in the ring. One day the circus owner made him appear with the elephant. But the elephant lost patience with the stupid donkey and sent him flying to the other side of the ring, and the whole act was spoilt.

The circus owner was so mad he
dragged the donkey to the edge of a

high cliff and pushed him over into the
sea where he was swallowed by a huge fish.

Now, as soon as Pinocchio was thrown
into the sea, the magician's spell was
broken. Inside the monster fish he was
his old self again.

"If only I had been true to the kind
Blue Fairy," he thought, as he began to
move about inside the huge dark body of
the fish. "I will never see her now."

Then he remembered the old man who
had made him. "He sold his coat so that
he could send me to school," Pinocchio
suddenly remembered. "And what did I do?
I ran away and he never saw me again."

As Pinocchio wandered along the fish's dark body something very strange and very wonderful happened. Who should he come upon but Geppetto, his dear father!

The old man was overcome with joy at the sight of his little wooden puppet. "I too was swallowed up by this monster fish," he told Pinocchio, "when my boat was sunk in a sudden storm."

For the first time in his short life
Pinocchio felt brave and confident. "I
will save you somehow, Father," he vowed.
As he spoke, the monster gave a great
fishy sneeze and they found themselves
shooting upwards. Then, lo and behold,
they were in the sea.

"Save yourself, Son," Geppetto cried.
"I cannot swim."

"Climb on my back," the little puppet
ordered. "The shore is not far."

Pinocchio struck out bravely for the
shore. But all too soon he began to grow
tired. Now he was swimming desperately,
using up all his strength. It was then

he saw the beautiful little goat again
– the very same he had seen just before
the monster fish had swallowed him.
The little goat's hair was not white or
black like the hair of other goats but
blue like that of the Blue Fairy.

The goat's presence on the rocks put fresh strength into the puppet and he reached the shore safely. "Lean on me, Father," Pinocchio said. "We cannot be far from the village…"

What joy for them both when they

found themselves at home. "I'll never
leave you again!" Pinocchio suddenly said.
As he spoke the Blue Fairy Girl was
there in the room. "Geppetto," she said
softly, "I come to give you a proper son,
a real, live boy with a heart of gold!"

Pinocchio and Geppetto lived together for many a long year. Pinocchio brought great happiness to the old man who took up his trade of wood-carving once again and began making lovely things out of wood.

To see the old man happy was all Pinocchio wanted. But he was happy too. His loving heart, given to him by the Blue Fairy, brought him many true friends.

"Would you believe it if I told you I was once a little wooden puppet?" he said to his best friend as they walked home from school one day. And his friend laughed and told him not to make silly remarks nobody would believe!

The Little Tin Soldier

Once upon a time there were twenty-five tin soldiers in a box. They were all brothers for they had all been made out of the same old tin spoon.

They looked very smart in their red and blue uniforms – even the soldier who had just one leg. You see, he had been made last and there just wasn't enough tin to give him two legs!

Every morning the soldiers were set out on the table with the Jack-in-the-box. Stiff and straight on his one leg, the tin soldier could see the pretty dancing girl. She stood in front of the cardboard castle, daintily poised on one slender leg. She too was made of cardboard but you would never have guessed it!

The little tin
soldier could not
take his eyes off
the pretty dancing
girl and soon he
had fallen deeply
in love with her.
"How beautiful she
is," he sighed. "I
know she is just the
very wife for me! But how can I ask her
to marry me? I am only a poor soldier."

As the days passed the tin soldier
fell more and more in love with the
pretty dancing girl. But he was far
too shy to speak to her about his love.
Then one day something truly dreadful
happened. The boy
stood his faithful
one-legged tin
soldier on the
window-ledge. The
window flew open
and down, down, down
fell the soldier
head first and still
clutching his musket.

The boy and his sister ran out to look
for him. "He must be somewhere," said
the boy. "Keep looking..."

"I can't see him anywhere," said his
sister. "Where can he be?"

Now the little tin soldier wasn't far
away. He could have cried out but he had
a soldier's courage and besides he was in
uniform. He must be extra brave!

The children searched a long time
for the brave little tin soldier who had
landed head first between the paving
stones, with his one leg stiff and
straight in the air.

When it started to rain, the boy
cried, "Come on! We can't look any
longer. Let's go inside and play one
of our games."

The little girl was sad to leave the
soldier out in the rain but she agreed.

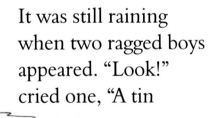

It was still raining
when two ragged boys
appeared. "Look!"
cried one, "A tin

soldier on his head. Let's give him a
chance to see the world by boat."

The boys searched around until they found some sheets of old newspaper which were dry enough to make into a boat.

"Are you sure it's going to be able to ride the waves?" asked the boy who was watching his friend make the boat. "Think of all the storms that lie ahead."

"Of course it is," came the reply. "Our soldier is going to have a great voyage."

When the boat was ready they put the tin soldier in it and away he sailed down the broad gutter.

"Good luck!" shouted one of the boys. "You'll see the world."

"Better keep your powder dry, soldier!" cried his friend, laughing loudly.

The brave tin soldier stood very erect on his one leg as the boat was tossed this way and that.

Sometimes he felt so dizzy and so sea-sick that it was a wonder he did not tumble overboard. But thoughts of his pretty dancing girl filled him with courage and he kept his eyes in front and a firm hold on his musket.

"Is this the end?" the soldier asked himself, as the paper boat suddenly began spinning round and round before entering a dark tunnel. "How black it is!"
For some reason he began thinking about his twenty-four brothers and the dark cardboard box which had once been home to them all.

Now the tunnel was where a tribe of fierce water-rats lived. Every day a guard was posted to question all new arrivals to their tunnel.

The tin soldier gave no sign that he had heard the harsh command of the rat on duty to stop.

"Stop and show me your passport!" screeched the guard as the boat sailed on.

Ahead of him the soldier could see daylight and, as the tunnel suddenly came to an end, his boat was tossed into the deep waters of the great canal.

"Nothing can save me now!" he gasped, as the paper boat fell apart and he was thrown into the swirling waters.

But almost at once the tin soldier was swallowed by a large fish.

How dark it was! And there was so little space inside the fish that he could scarcely move.

That day the big fish with the tin soldier inside it was no match for a patient fisherman.

"It's the best we've ever landed!" exclaimed his son in delight.

On the way to the market, father and son talked about what they would do after they had sold their fish.

The boy pleaded to be taken to the Fair but his father shook his head, saying they would go straight home.

The market was crowded and when the
fisherman proudly held up his prize
fish, there was no lack of buyers. He
asked the highest price he dared and it
was soon sold to one of his regular
customers who he knew well.

The cook was pleased to have the task of cooking such a fine fish. But when she cut it open - imagine her surprise!

Inside was the one-legged tin soldier! "Bless my soul!" she exclaimed, holding him up. "I've seen you before. You belong to the young master!"

The tin soldier had such a fishy smell that the first thing the cook did was to wash him in soapy water.

Then, after drying him on a clean kitchen towel, she carried him upstairs.

"That's the oddest story I've ever heard," said the boy's mother. "We buy the fish in the market and inside is my son's long-lost tin soldier!"

The boy was pleased to have his tin soldier back. "You'll keep guard tonight with your brothers!" he cried. "And guard the castle tomorrow."

The brave little tin soldier could scarcely believe his good fortune. After all his terrible adventures – here he was safely back with his brothers, and in the morning he would see his dancing girl. "I shall ask her to be my wife," he said to himself, his heart beating wildly.

Next day, the tin soldier went on
guard. Nothing had changed. The castle
was as splendid as he remembered it. The
swans were on the pond as usual.

The tin soldier fixed his eyes on the
dancing girl. "She is just as lovely as
she ever was," he thought. "I will ask
her to be my wife as soon as I go off-duty!"

Who knows why the boy should suddenly cast his tin soldier into the fire?
Or why, in the same moment, the dainty little dancing girl, caught up in a puff of wind, should follow him into the bright flames?

The brave little tin soldier and the pretty dancing girl in his arms melted together in the heat of the fire.

Soon, all too soon, they were gone. Only a lump of dull grey metal and a gold flower, worn by the dancing girl at her waist were left behind!

ISBN 0-86163-550-7
Copyright ©1992 Award Publications Limited
First Published 1992 Award Publications Limited,
Spring House, Spring Place, Kentish Town, London NW5 3BH
Printed in Singapore
Second impression 1993